Mack

Saddle Up Series
Book 39

Dave and Pat Sargent are longtime residents of Prairie Grove, Arkansas. Dave, a fourth-generation dairy farmer, began writing in early December 1990. Pat, a former teacher, began writing shortly after. They enjoy the outdoors and have a real love for animals.

Mack

Saddle Up Series
Book 39

By Dave and Pat Sargent

Beyond "The End"
By Sue Rogers

Illustrated by Jane Lenoir

Ozark Publishing, Inc.
P.O. Box 228
Prairie Grove, AR 72753

Cataloging-in-Publication Data

Sargent, Dave, 1941–
    Mack / by Dave and Pat Sargent ;
illustrated by Jane Lenoir.—Prairie Grove, AR :
Ozark Publishing, c2004.
    p. cm. (Saddle up series ; 39)

    "Be a leader"—Cover.
    SUMMARY: In 1805, an enthusiastic
horse carries Sacajawea, the Shoshone woman
hired to guide the Lewis and Clark Expedition,
from Fort Mandan to the Pacific Ocean. Includes
factual information about medicine hat paint
horses.
    ISBN 1-56763-699-3 (hc)
            1-56763-700-0 (pbk)
    1. Horses—Juvenile fiction. 2. Sacajawea,
1786–1884—Juvenile fiction. 3. Lewis and
Clark Expedition (1804–1806)—Juvenile
fiction. [1. Sacajawea, 1786–1884—Fiction.
2. Horses— Fiction. 3. Shoshoni Indians—
Fiction. 4. Indians of North America—Fiction.
5. Lewis and Clark Expedition (1804-1806)—
Fiction.] I. Sargent, Pat, 1936– II. Lenoir,
Jane, 1950– ill. III. Title. IV. Series.
    PZ7.S2465Mac 2004
    [Fic]—dc21   2001005619

iv

Inspired by

spotted medicine hat paints we see.

Dedicated to

all children who love spotted ponies.

Foreword

Mack's boss lady is Sacajawea, who has been hired, with the help of her medicine hat paint, to guide the Lewis and Clark Expedition through uncharted territory. When Mack hears a roar, Sacajawea nudges him with her moccasin-covered feet, and he lopes toward it. But when he sees what it is, he skids to a halt!

Contents

If you would like to have the authors of the Saddle Up Series visit your school, free of charge, call 1-800-321-5671 or 1-800-960-3876.

One

Boss Lady Sacajawea

The bellow of a bugle echoed within the confines of Fort Mandan. The loud wake-up call shattered the peaceful silence of early morning. Mack the medicine hat paint turned his ears from the noise and pawed the ground with one front hoof.

With a shake of his head, he snorted, "As long as I live, I'll never get used to the white man's way of waking up. Why, a rooster crowing or a hound dog baying could do a much better job."

1

The cavalry horses in the corral chuckled. Mack only glared at them.

"No Shoshone brave, squaw, papoose, or pony should be forced to listen to that racket first thing in the morning," he neighed loudly.

"It isn't a racket, Mack," the red sorrel explained. "That's the United States Cavalry saying it's time to get up and start the day."

"Humph!" Mack complained. "Any man, woman, child, or horse can tell that if they look toward the eastern horizon. The sun will peek through the trees to tell us the time."

Moments later, the fort was bustling with activity. Mack smiled when he saw Sacajawea walking toward him.

"Good morning, Boss Lady," he nickered.

The Shoshone Indian woman stroked his neck and whispered, "Mack, we will be leaving today. Meriwether Lewis and William Clark are ready to continue their expedition through uncharted territory. You and I, my medicine hat paint, will show them the way."

"Great, Boss Lady!" Mack neighed. "I'm ready to go to work."

Almost two hours later, Mack and Sacajawea were leading the Lewis and Clark Expedition through the newly acquired Louisiana Purchase territory.

"Hmmm," Mack murmured. "This is a new adventure for all of us." As the sun disappeared below the western horizon, Mr. Lewis loped his chocolate chestnut beside Mack and reined him to a halt.

"Sacajawea," he said. "It's time to stop for the night. I must write in my journals before it gets too dark to see. The United States government would not be pleased if I did not chart our route and findings each day."

Mack turned his head toward the chocolate chestnut. "This is going to be a good journey," he said. "We don't have to hurry, and we stop early in the evening."

"I sure hope your boss knows what she is doing," the chocolate chestnut said. "My boss said that she was taken from her people as a child and hasn't been back to her homeland since. Humph!" he added with a snort. "And now the Lewis and Clark Expedition is depending on your boss lady for a guide."

Mack glared at the chestnut before growling, "If Boss Lady says she can do it, she can do it!"

"Okay, okay," the chestnut said. "You don't need to get so testy."

"Let me tell you something," Mack warned. "Don't say anything but good about my boss lady."

That night, the medicine hat paint was dozing peacefully when he suddenly heard someone walking toward him. Then he heard the voice of his boss lady.

"Shhh," she hissed softly. "I cannot sleep, Mack. I need to talk to you for a little while. A strange thing is happening to me."

"Are you feeling okay, Boss?" Mack whispered.

Sacajawea sat down on a log. For a full minute she did not speak.

Mack nuzzled her on the cheek with his upper lip and whispered, "What's the matter, Boss Lady? The journey to your homeland seems to be going good. What's wrong?"

Sacajawea stroked Mack on his neck and smiled. "A strange thing is happening. I was very small when I last traveled through this territory, Mack, but my heart tells me every step to take. I will be seeing my people again very soon." Sacajawea smiled as she added, "I just can't explain to Mr. Lewis or Mr. Clark how I am finding the way."

"This is our secret, Boss Lady," Mack murmured. "Just keep up the good guide work. I am very proud of you."

Two

Shoshone Indian Camp

Seven days later, Mack and Sacajawea led the Lewis and Clark Expedition into the Shoshone Indian camp.

The medicine hat paint felt proud and very happy as he watched Sacajawea and her brother greet each other. Later that same evening, Mr. Lewis and Mr. Clark wrote in their journals, and Mack listened to the brother and sister talk.

The brother hugged Sacajawea and said, "I am sad to tell you that

our family is dead. The only ones
left are me and our sister's child."

    A tear slid down Mack's cheek.
He brushed it away on his front leg.

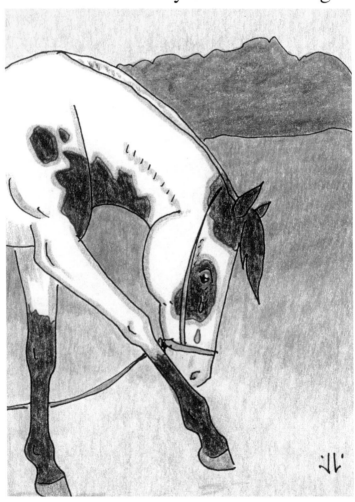

"Tell me what happened to you, my sister, after you left our camp?"

Sacajawea hesitated a moment before explaining, "A Frenchman named Toussaint Charbonneau won me in a gambling game. We got married shortly after that. And now Toussaint and I are hired as guides for the Lewis and Clark Expedition to explore America."

The big moon was high in the heavens when Mack yawned. "They will probably talk all night long," he thought. "Boss Lady's brother will take good care of her. I think I better lie down before I go to sleep and fall on someone." A moment later, he was snoring peacefully.

For many weeks after leaving the Shoshone Indian camp, Mack the medicine hat paint and Sacajawea quietly led the expedition through the untamed wilderness. With each passing day, notes were written in journals about the uncharted land. With each entry, the journals became more valuable to the new nation. One afternoon the party arrived at the edge of a big river.

"I must take good care of the journals," Mr. Clark said. "We will take them across the water in a canoe, and they will stay dry."

Mack and Sacajawea nodded their heads in agreement. Mr. Lewis and Mr. Clark carefully loaded the papers into the canoe with them. As it drifted toward the center of the river, a large log floating down the river banged against the side of the boat. Water began pouring through a hole that had been torn in its hull.

"Help!" the two men yelled. "We can swim, but the papers are floating away! We must save them!"

Mack's ears shot forward, and he leaped into the river. "Hang on, Boss Lady," he neighed. "I'll get you close. You grab the journals."

Sacajawea held tightly to his mane while Mack strained to swim against the moving water. Just as he swam beside the sinking craft, she reached out as far as she could.

"I have the papers, Mack," she screamed. "Hurry to the other side!"

Mack swam as fast as his legs could move in the rushing river. He was breathing hard and fast as he struggled up the bank onto dry land.

"You did it, Sacajawea!" both men yelled. "You and your Indian hat paint saved all of our journals!"

16

That evening beside the campfire, Mr. Lewis again thanked Mack and Sacajawea for their heroic deed.

"Sacajawea, the United States is grateful to both you and your medicine hat paint," he said. "And Mr. Clark and I are extremely proud that you two are members of our expedition."

Mack had a wonderful dream that night. In his vision, he and Sacajawea were presented with gold medals. The gold medallions were hanging from red ribbons, and the President of the United States slipped one over each of their necks.

The President said, "Mack, you earned this for your heroic deed in saving the Lewis and Clark journals. Without the journals, America would remain an uncharted land."

Mack heard a familiar voice, but he tried to ignore it. He did not want the dream to end, so he kept his eyes closed in hopes the vision would come true.

"Mack," the voice repeated. "Wake up. It is time to start a new day. We have many miles to travel."

"Good morning, Boss Lady," he said sheepishly. "I must have over-slept."

"We had a great day yesterday, Mack," she said. "Perhaps we will find another new adventure on this fine day."

"Wow!" Mack said excitedly. "What a neat way to start the day. Let's go, Boss Lady."

Three

Lewis and Clark Expedition

For another month, the Lewis and Clark Expedition continued to travel westward. The medicine hat paint and Sacajawea carefully led them beside rivers that wound through mountains, woodlands, and flatlands.

Late one afternoon Mack was walking in tall lush grass when he suddenly heard a strange sound. Seconds later, the quiet and peaceful afternoon was shattered by a loud and very frightened yelp.

Sacajawea was more curious than frightened. She asked, "Mack, what is that?"

"I am not sure," he nickered softly. "But I intend to find out."

As Mack trotted toward the mysterious noise, Mr. Lewis yelled, "Be careful, Sacajawea. You and Mack let us check on the problem. It may be a bear."

"We will be careful," she said as she nudged Mack into a lope.

"Right," the medicine hat paint said. "Boss Lady and I will check into this. We can handle anything that comes up."

Fifteen minutes later, the paint and his boss lady found an Indian boy accidentally caught in a game trap. The boy looked terrified as the horse and rider approached.

Sacajawea soothed the child with soft words as she cut away the leaves and limbs. Mack chewed the leather thongs that held the boy.

Suddenly, a voice startled them.

"That is my son," a very tall Indian chief said in a deep voice. "Do not hurt him."

Sacajawea held the boy's hand as he slipped to the ground from the trap.

"We will not hurt your son," she said quietly. "He was caught in your game trap, and we helped him get loose."

Sacajawea and the Indian chief visited for nearly an hour.

"I wish to thank you and your Mack horse for saving my son," he said. "You and your friends will eat with us tonight. I am most anxious to meet with your friends, Mr. Lewis and Mr. Clark."

Later that night, Mack nuzzled his boss lady on the cheek as he murmured, "You are more than a guide for Lewis and Clark. You are also a United States diplomat on Indian relations. Good job, Boss!"

With each passing day, the expedition learned new information about the untamed land of America.

On November 7, 1805, Mack and Sacajawea heard a strange roar. Sacajawea nudged Mack with her moccasin-covered feet, and he loped toward the noise. As he reached the crest of a hill, he skidded to a halt.

"Good grief!" he neighed. "I can't see anything but water. Wow! Look at those big waves."

Sacajawea laughed and said, "Mack, this is the Pacific Ocean. We have reached our destination."

The entire Lewis and Clark Expedition rested and relaxed on the beach for several days.

Mr. Lewis and Mr. Clark sat down on the beach and wrote in their journals as Mack and Sacajawea explored the tideline and swam in the ocean. The sun was high overhead one day when Mack stopped playing and watched Sacajawea.

"I'm proud of you, Boss Lady," he nickered.

"Hmmm," he thought. "One day the whole world will know about my boss leading the Lewis and Clark Expedition to the Pacific Ocean. Sacajawea will be written about in history books. I wonder if folks will remember her medicine hat paint named Mack. Oh well. I really don't care. Each and every day with Sacajawea is a big and exciting adventure!"

Four

Medicine Hat Paint Facts

Medicine hat paint is the name cowboys give to horses that are mostly all white with a pattern of color on the ears, sometimes with colored patches on the chest, flank, and base of the tail.

The medicine hat is not really a separate pattern of white spotting. It is a name cowboys use for the way the colored areas are placed on a mostly white horse.

The colored patches on the ears are called the "bonnet," and the patches on the body are like "war shields."

Medicine Hat Paint

War bonnet paints have very similar coloring on the ears but very little on the body. Horses with these markings were thought by some tribes of Indians to be imbued with supernatural powers.

Overo

Overos, which are mostly white, and horses on which the overo and tobiano patterns are combined, are also thought to have supernatural powers. Sabinos that are mostly white are always this pattern, and so are sabino-overo combinations.

BEYOND "THE END"

Horses can't talk,
but they can speak if you listen!
Anonymous

Below are the names of the horses and bosses from ten books in the Saddle Up Series.

Horse:	Boss:
GUS	Harriet Tubman
MACK	Annie Trebble
NUBBIN	"Grand Canyon"
PETE	Sacajawea
RANGER	Daniel Boone
RASCAL	Allan Pinkerton
RUSTY	Dr. Rogers
SONNY	Slim (rodeo)
WHISKERS	Bat Masterson
ZEB	Chief Joseph

Write the words in the list on page 37 on a piece of paper. Match the name of the HORSE in the left column with the name of his or her BOSS in the right column.

CURRICULUM CONNECTIONS

Assign small research groups to gather information about each of the main characters in the Lewis and Clark Expedition. They will make their reports reflecting the individual contributions each character made to the Expedition. Main characters include the following:

Thomas Jefferson
Meriwether Lewis
William Clark
Private John Colter
Toussaint Charbonneau
Sacajawea
Jean Baptiste Charbonneau/Pomp

These websites are especially helpful: <www.pbs.org/lewisandclark> and <www.lewisandclarktrail.com> and <www.lewis-clark.org>.

The Lewis and Clark Expedition trail passes through portions of how many states?

Name the states.

How long is the trail?

PROJECT

Combine your math and artistic skills! Draw to scale and accurately color a picture (body, tail, and mane) of the horse that is featured in each book read in the Saddle Up Series. You could soon have sixty horses prancing around the walls of your classroom!
Learning + horses = FUN.

Look in your school library media center for books about how to draw a horse and the colors of horses. Don't forget the useful information in the last chapter of this book (Medicine Hat Paint Facts) and the picture on the book cover for a shape and color guide.

HELPFUL HINTS AND WEBSITES
A horse is measured in hands. One hand equals four inches. Use a scale of 1" equals 1 hand.

More information can be found at <www.horse-country.com> and at Visit website <www.equisearch.com> to find a glossary of equine terms, information about tack and equipment, breeds, art and graphics, and more about horses. Learn more at <www.horse-country. com> and at <www.ansi.okstate.edu/breeds/horses/>.

KidsClick! is a web search for kids by librarians. There are many interesting websites here. HORSES and HORSE-MANSHIP are two of the more than 600 subjects. Visit <www.kidsclick.org>.

Is your classroom beginning to look like the Rocking S Horse Ranch? Happy Trails to You!

ANSWERS (11 states: IA, ID, IL, KS, MO, MT, ND, NE, OR, SD, and WA. 3,700 miles long.)